HEDGEHOGS

SAVIOUR PIROTTA

A Giant Stepped on Joey's Toe

illustrated by
Larry Wilkes

HODDER AND STOUGHTON
London Sydney Auckland Toronto

British Library Cataloguing in Publication Data

Pirotta, Saviour
  A giant stepped on Joey's toe.
  I. Title   II. Wilkes, Larry   III. Series
  823'.914 [J]

  ISBN 0-340-51426-4

Published by Hodder and Stoughton Children's Books,
a division of Hodder and Stoughton Ltd,
Mill Road, Dunton Green, Sevenoaks, Kent TN13 2YA

Photoset by En to En, Tunbridge Wells, Kent

Printed in Great Britain by Cambus Litho, East Kilbride

Joey and his three brothers lived on a farm.
Joey's brothers were big and macho.
Every Monday they went to karate
lessons.

Every Tuesday they practised their shooting and their fencing.

Wednesdays they jogged and did push-ups to increase their strength.

The rest of the week they ate healthy meals and lifted weights to make their muscles grow bigger.

Joey spent most of his spare time learning to play the violin.

'That fiddle sounds dreadful. It's like a yowling cat,' the brothers complained.
'You should learn boxing instead, Joey. It will come in more useful than playing a violin.'

One morning, while Joey was polishing his violin, a terrible roar shook the farm.

'Who's that?' the brothers growled dangerously.

Joey rushed to the window. 'It's a giant!' he gasped.

The brothers pushed him aside to have a look. Right in the middle of their field, they saw a hairy giant pulling up their trees.

'Food,' bellowed the giant. 'Hungry.' And he gobbled up a conker tree in one gulp.

'I'll give him hungry if he doesn't get off our property at once,' Joey's eldest brother fumed. 'I'll chop him to bits with my bare hands.'

The other brothers cheered. 'Go on,' they said. 'Bash him up.'

The giant heard them and looked up. 'Humans,' he roared happily. 'Yum-yum.'

'That does it,' Joey's eldest brother said.
'Nobody says yum-yum to my face.
I'm going to thrash him.'

'Wait,' Joey cried. 'Maybe the fellow
doesn't know they're our trees.'

'Nonsense,' said the eldest brother.
He stomped out to the field with his hands
waving in the air. 'He-aah,' he screamed at
the giant. 'Hoy-yey. Miaaaoow.'

The giant grinned. 'Goo-goo,' he said.
'Goo-goo.'

'I'll give you goo-goo,' snarled Joey's brother as he raised his foot and struck the giant in the knee.

For a second the giant looked puzzled. Then, thinking this was a game, he grinned and stepped playfully on the brother's toe.

'Ouch,' cried the brother. 'That's cheating.'

The giant grinned again. He sucked in his breath and blew the man straight back into the house.

'I'll deal with the pest,' gloated the second brother.

He fetched two swords and marched out into the field. 'On guard,' he called, throwing one of the swords at the giant's feet. '*Touché.*'

The giant smiled. He picked up the sword and looked at it carefully. Then he started to pick his teeth with it.

'Fight, you big oaf,' snarled the second brother.

Angrily, he pricked the giant's big knee with his sword. The giant looked as if he was going to cry. Sulkily, he raised his foot and stepped on the second brother's toe.

'That's against the rules,' the second brother protested.

The giant sighed impatiently. He bit on the sword and broke it in two. The second brother hobbled back to the farm as fast as he could.

'It looks as if I'll have to deal with the pest, then,' the third brother boasted. 'Where's my gun?'

'You can't shoot him,' Joey gasped.

'Can't I?' laughed the brother wickedly as he hurried across the field. 'Hands up,' he ordered the giant.

The giant seemed to have lost his patience now. 'Agoo—,' he mumbled angrily.

The third brother raised his gun. Carefully he drew back the hammer. He pulled the trigger.

Bang! A blast of fire leapt from the gun. At the same time the giant bared his teeth. The bullet bounced off his gnashing molars.

'Help! I'm out of ammunition,' the third brother cried.

Before he could run away, the giant
stepped on his toe and snatched him up.
　'Watch out,' Joey cried from the window,
'he's coming to get us next.'

The brothers leapt to shut the window.
But the giant got to it before them. His hand
swept into the room and grabbed them all
up.

'Mum-my,' the three brothers wailed.

'Stop it,' Joey scolded. 'I think I know how
to calm this giant down.' He put the violin
under his chin and tried to play 'Silent Night'.

All at once the giant froze.

'You're setting his teeth on edge,' moaned
the eldest brother. 'Stop it.'

Joey smiled and played a little bit louder.
The violin screeched horribly, like someone
scraping their nails down a blackboard.

'Shut it,' begged the brothers with their
hands over their ears.

Joey's only answer was to play faster. Soon the giant's hair was standing on end. His eyes bulged.

Joey finished 'Silent Night' and started on 'Happy Birthday to You'. At last the giant couldn't take it any more. He dropped the brothers on a haystack and covered his ears with his hands.

'I can play "God Save the Queen",' Joey grinned proudly. 'Watch.'

The brothers didn't stay to listen. They leapt off the haystack and darted back into the house.

The giant was visibly trembling now. As he stood there, his trousers slid to the ground. Joey burst out laughing. Immediately, the giant saw his chance and stepped on his toe.

'Oww!' Joey jumped. The violin flew up in the air. The giant caught it. Then, without bothering to pick up his trousers, he ran away beyond the hills.

'He's pinched my violin,' Joey shouted.

'Good for him,' said the brothers ungratefully, quite forgetting that it was Joey who had chased the giant away.

The brothers fixed themselves a foot-bath. The fight with the giant had tired them out. They needed a nice long rest . . .

Suddenly, a horrible noise like the sound of a castle door creaking on rusty hinges made them wince.

'What's that?' they cried.

'The giant is learning the violin now,' Joey
laughed. 'And look, he's brought a drum
with him. I bet it's for me.'

And it was. Joey and the giant played
'Silent Night' all day.